TWIDDLEBUGS AT WORK

Featuring Jim Henson's Sesame Street Muppets

by Linda Hayward
Illustrated by Irene Trivas

A SESAME STREET/GOLDEN PRESS BOOK
Published by Western Publishing Company, Inc.
in conjunction with Children's Television Workshop.

Library of Congress Catalog Card Number: 80-50850
ISBN 0-307-23115-1

Do you know about Twiddlebugs? Twiddlebugs live in window boxes. In fact, there is an entire Twiddlebug town in Ernie's window box, and he doesn't even know it.

And what do Twiddlebugs do all day? If you think that they just sit around and twiddle, you are mistaken. Twiddlebugs only sit around and twiddle at night. During the day they work!

window
washer

dressmaker

OFFICE BUILDING

road
worker

They work indoors.
They work outdoors.
They work up high.
They work down low.
Twiddlebugs are always working to make
Twiddlebug Town a nice place to live.

designer

delivery bug

assembly line workers

packers

loader

Some of the Twiddlebugs work in factories, making the things that Twiddlebugs need, such as furniture and clothing. These factory workers are making Twiddle toys.

sales clerk

customer

Twiddlebug BAKERY

pastry cook

baker

FLOUR

Down the street is a bakery where Twiddle bakers make bread for Twiddlebugs to eat. They make corn bread, rye bread, wheat bread, gingerbread and Twiddle tarts. In the bakery shop a Twiddlebug can buy a Twiddle birthday cake.

Next door there is a restaurant. The cook in the kitchen is making a delicious pea soup.

CLANG! CLANG! CLANG!
The alarm is ringing at the fire station.
There is a fire on Main Street! The Twiddlebug
fire fighters jump into their fire engines.
Off they go!

fire fighters

The trash in the back of a garbage truck
is burning. Luckily, none of the trash collectors
is hurt. The fire fighters will put out the flames.

fire
chief

fire
fighter

trash
collectors

police
officer

street
cleaner

The Twiddlebugs who did not see the fire can read about it in the newspaper. The Twiddle Times photographer took a picture of the burning truck and the Twiddle Times reporter will write a story about it.

There is a hospital in Twiddlebug Town.
The doctors and nurses at the hospital take care of
sick Twiddlebugs and make them feel better.

Next door is a building full of doctor's offices.
The doctors help Twiddlebugs stay healthy. They check
their eyes, ears and wings.

electrician

plumber

plasterer

When Twiddlebugs move to Twiddlebug Town, they sometimes need a new house. The carpenters build the house. The plumber puts in the pipes, the electrician does the wiring, and the painters paint the house a nice Twiddlebug color.

baggage
handler

Twiddlebugs like to travel. The Twiddlebugs
who work at the airport and on the airplanes make
the travelers comfortable and safe.

passengers

The Twiddlebug travelers send postcards home from faraway window boxes.

Some Twiddlebugs work at the post office. They take care of all the postcards and letters that the Twiddlebugs write. They weigh them, stamp them, sort them, and deliver them.

After work, the Twiddlebugs go home. On the way, some of them stop to shop at the store.

GENERAL STORE

cashier

TOYS

BIG GIRL